10/04

Juan Díaz
CANALES
Writer

Juanjo
GUARNIDO
Artist and Colorist

SOMEWHERE WITHIN THE SHADOWS

Introduction by
STERANKO

ibooks

graphic novel

www.ibooks.net
www.komikwerks.com
DISTRIBUTED BY SIMON & SCHUSTER

(GRAPH)

BLACKSAD

311-8174

Also in this series
BLACKSAD—Arctic Nation
by Canales and Guarnido

TO OUR PARENTS

An ibooks, inc. graphic novel

Distributed by Simon & Schuster, Inc.
1230 Avenue of the Americas, New York, NY 10020

ibooks, inc.
24 West 25th Street
New York, NY 10010

The ibooks graphic novels World Wide Web Site address is:
http://www.komikwerks.com

Cover Art: Juanjo Guarnido
Translated by Anthya Flores & Patricia Rivera
Cover and Interior Design: Arnie Sawyer Studios, Inc.

www.dargaud.com

First ibooks edition December 2003
ISBN: 0-7434-7991-2

10 9 8 7 6 5 4 3 2

STERANKO

Introduction by

BLACKSAD

If it's true that cats have nine lives, then Blacksad must have a few dozen.

While there's a long, aesthetic tradition of animals in the comics, Guarnido and Canales are obviously in the process of establishing their own tradition. Initially defined by the term funny animals—which suggests a range between cute and cuddly—the genre was never quite devoid of sledgehammer violence, mysterious doings, and sometimes even a little sex. And that was previous to the liberation of the form in the 1960s, after which four-footed creatures behaved more like real people than most comic book characters—thanks to Crumb and company.

Blacksad takes the trend to another level. Rather than animals who act like people, the creators' approach is predicated on people who resemble animals. There's a major difference and it's not as remote as it seems. Who hasn't likened a shrill librarian to a bird or a construction worker to a bear or an old aunt to a cow? By animalizing their characters, Guarnido and Canales invite readers to enter an area where the animals are somewhat less than funny, one that's relatively easy to accept because the premise is so charming and skillfully conceived, not unlike James Gurney's *Dinotopia* or Bob Zemekis' *Who Framed Roger Rabbit?*

In Blacksad's world, the characters are generally unconcerned about their zoological differences; they are cast for their natures and personalities. To the perceptive reader, it's almost impossible not to see a trace of slinky Lauren Bacall in Natalia Wilford or burly Ernie Borgnine in Jake Ostiombe or slippery James Woods in the lizard. It's no accident that, down to the last bit player, they've all been crafted visually to reflect their intrinsic qualities—which might just qualify as overt symbolism. Or simple typecasting.

While his draftsmanship is as superb as it is appealing, Guarnido's sharpest and most persuasive ability is apparent in the emotional nuances and facial expressions of his characters, easily the equal of any Disney effort on record. There is a compelling maturity about his art that seems to invest his anthropomorphic cast with experience, vitality, and even dignity. He gets more out of his animal faces than most artists do from people faces. The trick, of course, is making it look easy, like a trapeze artist who throws a triple so flawlessly that the audience believes they could do it, too.

That is no easy task. Here's the universal equation: the easier it looks, the more study, the more practice, the more dedication it takes.

The real pros, however, never allow their relentless quest for discipline and sacrifice to show. But it's there, if you know how to look for it. And while you're looking, don't miss the interesting narrative approach that Guarnido lavishes on his pages, an amalgam of traditional European comics story-telling and American cinematic style. The latter is a critical aspect in the artist's vision and one he leans heavily on in both concept and execution.

Blacksad's adventures are, in many ways, like films on paper. Canales taps into the dark heart of stateside noir thrillers (not to suggest that Europe, especially France, doesn't have its fair share) for his structural elements: first-person narration, revealing flashbacks, and a nightmarish chiaroscuro of predatory characters in stark silhouette, cluttered offices, grids of vene-tian blinds, shadowy stairwells, and architectural canyons of iron and con-crete illuminated by a maze of flashing neon.

Classic noir themes developed in the pulps by Hammett, Chandler, Goodis, Whitfield, Nebel, Woolrich, and Cain, among others, are manifest in Blacksad's search for justice. His bitter manhunt thrusts him through a gauntlet of corruption, betrayal, obsessive sexuality, alienation, and revenge that mirrors the most memorable genre efforts of RKO and Warner Bros. during the era of black & white B movies.

Particularly notable are Guarnido's muted color passages, giving the impression of the '40s and '50s crime thrillers that have come to define the noir experience. His use of light and shadow is no less memorable, and he often utilizes illumination—sometimes the lack of it—to underscore the drama twisting Blacksad through an urban landscape riddled with mystery, violence, and passion.

Curiosity may have killed some cats,
but not this one.

He's too tough.
STERANKO

THERE ARE MORNINGS WHEN ONE HAS TROUBLE DIGESTING HIS BREAKFAST... ESPECIALLY IF YOU FIND YOURSELF IN FRONT OF THE DEAD BODY OF AN OLD FLAME...

...THE REMAINS OF A BEAUTIFUL DREAM.

DO YOU RECOGNIZE HER?

YES. DID YOU FIND SOMETHING?

ABSOLUTELY NOTHING. NO WEAPON, NO MOTIVE, NO SUSPECT....

I THOUGHT YOU COULD HELP US....

I HADN'T SEEN HER FOR A LONG TIME...

...TOO LONG.

ALL RIGHT. THANKS FOR COMING. YOU MAY LEAVE NOW.

I CAN SEE THAT THIS WASN'T A ROBBERY.

LISTEN TO ME, BLACKSAD, AND PAY ATTENTION. FOR EVERYBODY'S SAKE, FOLLOW MY ADVICE AND KEEP YOUR MUZZLE OUT OF THIS CASE.

DO YOU UNDERSTAND, BLACKSAD?

GO TO HELL, SMIRNOV.

SOMETIMES, WHEN I WALK INTO MY OFFICE, I GET THE IMPRESSION THAT I'M WALKING AMONG THE RUINS OF A LOST CIVILIZTION. NOT BECAUSE OF THE REIGNING DISORDER, BUT BECAUSE IT ALL SEEMS TO BE THE REMAINS OF THAT CIVILIZED PERSON THAT I USED TO BE.

BUT ALL THAT WAS IN THE PAST. A PAST THAT WAS STARING BACK AT ME FROM THE FRONT PAGE OF THE NEWSPAPER...

FAMOUS ACTRESS NATALIA WILFORD MURDERED AT HOME

"...A STAR."

THOUGH NATALIA DIDN'T SHINE LIKE A STAR THE FIRST TIME I MET HER. ON THE CONTRARY HER FACE DIDN'T REFLECT ANYTHING ELSE, EXCEPT...

... THE PALENESS OF FEAR.

3

I FOUND IT WEIRD THAT SOMEBODY WOULD BE SO WORRIED ABOUT RECEIVING SO MANY EXPRESSIONS OF LOVE AND ADMIRATION FROM HER FANS...

Enjoy your flowers and the last days of your life, BITCH!

To the most beautiful of future corpses

UNTIL I READ THOSE CARDS:

THE TASK WAS TO DO THE JOB IN A DISCRETE AND EFFICIENT WAY. AND WHEN I PUT MY MIND TO IT, I CAN BE VERY DISCRETE, AND INDEED...

EFFICIENT.

SHE WAS IMPRESSED WITH THE RESULTS.

SO MUCH THAT SHE DECIDED TO KEEP ME AT HER SERVICES.

THOSE WERE THE HAPPIEST DAYS OF MY LIFE....

5

BUT THE GODDESS WAS HUMAN, AND NO DIFFERENT FROM EVERYBODY ELSE, WITH HER PROBLEMS, EMOTIONS...

...ASPIRATIONS...

...AND WEAKNESSES.

AND, SINCE NOBODY'S PERFECT AND PERFECT LOVE DOESN'T EXIST...

CIRCUMSTANCES EVENTUALLY TOOK OVER AND TORE US APART.

SINCE THEN, I HADN'T SEEN HER...

...UNTIL TODAY.

A STAR HAD BEEN ECLIPSED, LEAVING MY PAST IN THE DARKNESS, LOST SOMEWHERE WITHIN THE SHADOWS. AND NOBODY CAN LIVE WITHOUT A PAST.

OUT THERE, HIDING SOMEWHERE, WAS THE GUILTY ONE. GUILTY OF AT LEAST TWO MURDERS, FOR HE HAD KILLED A PERSON AND MY MEMORIES.

AND THAT BASTARD WAS GOING TO PAY!

I DIDN'T HAVE A CLUE TO BEGIN WITH, SO I WENT TO VISIT JAKE OSTIOMBE, AN OLD FRIEND.

JAKE WAS A HEAVYWEIGHT THAT I HAD RECOMMENDED AS A BODYGUARD TO NATALIA...

...AND, FRANKLY, I BELIEVE IT WAS A GOOD IDEA.

I SEE YOU STILL HIT HARD, JAKE.

LET'S SAY THAT I DEFEND MYSELF. WHAT BRINGS YOU AROUND, JOHN?

IT'S ABOUT NATALIA. I'M INVESTIGATING HER DEATH AND I NEED SOMETHING TO BEGIN WITH.

THWOMP!

WELL, THERE AIN'T MUCH TO TELL. SHE FIRED ME LONG AGO. SHE SAID SHE DIDN'T NEED ME ANYMORE, THAT SHE HAD HER OWN SECURITY SERVICE.

IN FACT, THE TOUGH GUYS AROUND HER MUST HAVE BEEN PAID BY ONE OF HER MANY "ADMIRERS."

I SEE. AND, DO YOU REMEMBER THE NAME OF ONE OF THOSE "ADMIRERS"?

LAST ONE I HEARD ABOUT WAS SOME "LEON," BUT I DON'T REMEMBER NOTHING ELSE.

MEMORY AIN'T ONE OF MY STRONGER POINTS.

THAT'LL DO. THANK YOU, JAKE.

HEY, JOHN! AS YOU CAN SEE, SHE DIDN'T MISS YOU MUCH!

9

LEON KRONSKI, MOVIE SCRIPTWRITER.

THE NAME AND PROFESSION OF NATALIA'S LAST KNOWN LOVER.

IT SEEMED LIKE LEON HAD LEFT HOME IN A HURRY, LIKE RUNNING FROM SOMETHING , WHICH MADE HIM THE MAIN SUSPECT.

BUT SOMETHING DIDN'T FIT. THAT PLACE DIDN'T LOOK LIKE THE APARTMENT OF SOME ONE WHO COULD AFFORD A PRIVATE SECURITY SERVICE.

CLIC
CLAC

OH, MY GOODNESS!! YOU SCARED ME! BUT... WHO ARE YOU?

I'M A VERY CLOSE FRIEND OF MR. LEON... I HAVE THE KEYS TO THE APARTMENT SO I CAME TO PICK UP SOME BOOK THAT I'D LENT HIM, YOU KNOW, I'VE BEEN TRYING TO LOCATE HIM FOR DAYS WITHOUT ANY SUCCESS.

DO YOU KNOW IF HE'S LEFT TOWN?

YES, HE'S ON A TRIP... OR AT LEAST, THAT'S WHAT HIS OTHER FRIEND TOLD ME.

ANOTHER FRIEND?

WELL, THE TRUTH IS THAT I DON'T REMEMBER HIM SAYING HIS NAME...

BUT I DO REMEMBER THOSE BULGING EYES!

?

11

I TOLD YOU TO GET ME A SAX-OPHONIST...!

AND WHAT I HAVE HERE IS A XYLOPHONIST!!!

OF COURSE IT'S NOT THE SAME THING A SAXOPHONE AND A XYLOPHONE!

GO TO HELL!

AND DON'T PUT THROUGH ANY MORE CALLS THIS MORNING!

I'M SURROUNDED BY INCOMPETENTS!

MISS, DO ME A FAVOR AND TAKE THIS PERSON OUT OF MY SIGHT!

GIVE ME GOOD NEWS OR GET OUT!

GOOD MORNING, MR. ZENUCK. I'M J.H. BLACKMORE FROM "SMOKE AGENCY, DEBT COLLECTORS".

I'M LOOKING FOR A MR. LEON KRONSKI.... OBVIOUSLY CONCERNING A MONEY PROBLEM.

SO YOU'RE LOOKING FOR LEON! THEN PLEASE LET ME KNOW IF YOU FIND HIM!

AND...IF YOU NEED A CONTRIBUTION TO BREAK HIS LEGS, LET ME BE THE FIRST ONE ON YOUR LIST.

FIRST THE MAIN ACTRESS GETS MURDERED AND NOW THE SCRIPTWRITER RUNS AWAY!

UH... THEN...YOU DON'T KNOW WHERE HE IS?

OF COURSE NOT! HIS FRIEND, THE ONE WHO CAME TO TELL MY SECRETARY THAT LEON WAS LEAVING, DIDN'T SAY WHERE THE HELL HE WAS GOING!

A GUY WITH BULGING EYES?

13

DO YOU KNOW SON, I LOVE TO COLLECT INSECTS.

CLASSIFY, ORGANIZE...

... IT IS SO SATISFYING TO PUT EACH THING IN ITS PLACE. AND, DO YOU KNOW WHAT MAKES THIS HOBBY SO PLEASING?

NO, SIR.

OF COURSE YOU DON'T KNOW. I'M GOING TO TELL YOU; ITS USELESS-NESS, IT HAS NO PURPOSE, THAT'S THE BEAUTY OF IT; IF IT HAD A PURPOSE IT WOULD LOSE ITS CHARM.

16

THAT'S LIFE, WHEN SOMETHING STOPS BEING USEFUL... ZAP!!!

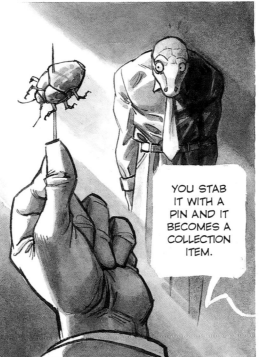

YOU STAB IT WITH A PIN AND IT BECOMES A COLLECTION ITEM.

WELL, I HOPE YOU GET THE IDEA. YOU CAN LEAVE NOW. AND LET ME TAKE CARE OF THAT CAT. YOU WORRY SO MUCH ABOUT IT THAT IT'S STARTING TO LOOK AS IF YOU HAVE SOMETHING PERSONAL AGAINST HIM.

THANK YOU, SIR.

LOYALTY... THAT'S ALL I'M ASKING, SON.

YOU'LL BE DOING ME A BIG FAVOR, IF YOU CATCH THE IN-SECT THAT JUST FLEW OUT THROUGH THAT DOOR. AM I WRONG OR DOES HE HAVE SOMETHING THAT BELONGS TO ME?

AH! AND CAREFUL WITH THE PINS.

17

25

HEY, BRO!

WHAT'S UP?

HELLO, BOYS.

DO YOU HAVE A CIGARETTE, BIG GUY?

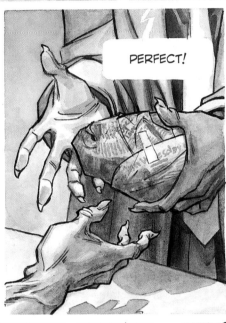

SCREEEEECH!..

J. GUARNIDO

TSCH, TSCH, TSCH....
I WOULD SAY YOU'RE
IN THE WRONG HOLE...

AÏÏÏK!

...PAL.

HAIRY GUYS LIKE
YOU ARE NOT VERY
WELCOME HERE.

GULP!

20

THE CYPHER CLUB WAS NOT KNOWN FOR ITS ELEGANCE.

TRUTHFULLY, IT WASN'T THE TYPE OF PLACE THAT NATALIA WOULD FREQUENT...

UNLESS SHE'D DONE IT TO PLEASE LEON, OR TO HIDE FROM SOMEBODY.

LET'S SEE... LEON, LEON...

GOT IT! HE WAS THE ONE WITH THAT STUNNING GIRL!

SHE MUST HAVE BEEN AN ACTRESS OR SOMETHING LIKE THAT, TAKE MY WORD FOR IT, I GOT THE EYE.

I SEE, AND WHAT ABOUT THAT GUY, LEON?

I'VE NO IDEA. THE TRUTH IS THAT IT'S BEEN SOME TIME SINCE THEY LAST CAME HERE.

HEY, FRIEND...!

COULDN'T HELP OVER-HEARING. YOU KNOW, I COULD TAKE YOU TO LEON...FOR A PRICE, OF COURSE!

I'M GOING DOWN TO THE CEMETERY 'COS THE WORLD IS ALL WRONG... DOWN THERE WITH THE SPOOK'S, TO HEAR 'EM SING MY SORROW SONG...

FROM THE BEGINNING I FELT A REPULSION FOR MY NEW "FRIEND"...

...A MATTER OF INSTINCT.

ANYWAY, THE RAT HAD HONORED HIS PART OF THE CONTRACT.

HE WAS THERE, RIGHT IN FRONT OF ME "THE GOOD OLD LEON."

RIP
NOEL KRISNOK
1916

MY SEARCH HAD COME TO AN END IN FRONT OF A SINISTER RIDDLE: NOEL KRISNOK WAS AN ANAGRAM OF LEON KRONSKY. TWO NAMES FOR ONE CORPSE.

WHAT POSSIBLE SIN COULD HE HAVE COMMITTED TO DESERVE DEATH? TO LOVE THE WRONG WOMAN?

IF THAT WAS THE CASE...

23

...I WAS DAMNED, TOO.

THE RAT HAD SLIPPED AWAY...

...INSTINCT IS ALMOST NEVER WRONG.

?

HEY, YOU, PRIVATE EYE. WE HAVE A MESSAGE FOR YOU.

PAF

24

HOW TO DESCRIBE THOSE GUYS?

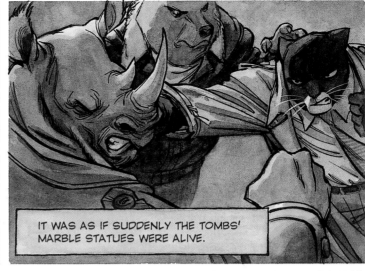

IT WAS AS IF SUDDENLY THE TOMBS' MARBLE STATUES WERE ALIVE.

AND NOT SO MUCH DUE TO THEIR SINISTER LOOKS, THAN TO THEIR HARDNESS.

TO PUNCH BACK WAS LIKE HITTING A STONE WALL.

EVEN THOUGH THERE IS A WORD WHICH WOULD DESCRIBE THEM PERFECTLY.

PROFESSIONALS.

HOPE YOU GOT THE MESSAGE. IF NOT, WE DON'T MIND REPEATING IT.

FUCK YOU....

PAF!

IDIOT!

I DON'T KNOW HOW LONG I REMAINED UNCONSCIOUS ON SACRED GROUNDS...

... WHAT I DO KNOW IS THAT WHEN I WOKE UP, I FELT A LITTLE AT HOME.

MUCH LATER, I FOUND MYSELF WANDERING TO MY APARTMENT WITH THE FEELING THAT I HAD AGED TWENTY YEARS IN ONLY A DAY.

BUT IN THIS CITY, NO ONE RESPECTS THE ELDERLY ANYMORE.

LYING BEATEN UP ON THAT COT, THE ONLY THING I STILL HAD WAS SOME SORT OF MENTAL AGILITY.

LEON, NATALIA'S LAST LOVER, HAD GONE UNDER A FAKE NAME ON A TRIP TO "SEE THE OTHER SIDE."

ELIMINATING AND ERASING THE TRACKS OF SOMEONE ISN'T SOMETHING THAT JUST ANYONE CAN DO. ONLY SOMEONE VERY POWERFUL CAN PERMIT HIMSELF THE LUXURY OF HAVING SOMEONE DIS-CREETLY MURDERED.

SOMEONE, BUT... WHO?

26

THE HUMIDITY SEEPED INTO MY BONES AND IT WOULDN'T BE TOO LONG BEFORE SMIRNOV STARTED CHEWING OFF WHAT WAS LEFT OF THEM. WITH SUCH AN APPEALING IMAGE, I FELL ASLEEP.

I DREAMT OF HER.

I WAS DEEPLY SAD IN THE MORNING.

GOOD MORNING, BLACKSAD.

COME IN AND GET COMFORTABLE, CHIEF. FEEL AT HOME.

I GUESS...

...YOU'RE CURIOUS TO KNOW WHY YOU'RE IN JAIL.

YOU SEE, SMIRNOV, I'M STARTING TO BELIEVE THAT OLD SAYING, "CURIOSITY KILLED THE CAT."

27

YOU KNOW, BLACKSAD, THE WILFORD CASE IS BEGINNING TO BE VERY DANGEROUS. I'VE ARRESTED YOU IN ORDER TO SPARE YOU SOME PROBLEMS.

AS YOU CAN SEE, YOU WERE A LITTLE LATE. THEY MADE A MAP OUT OF MY FACE.

BAH! THAT'S NOTHING. I DON'T THINK THAT BEING A LITTLE UGLIER FOR A TIME WOULD MATTER MUCH. A CIGARETTE?

DON'T PUT ON THAT POKER FACE, JOHN. I HAVE SOMETHING VERY IMPORTANT TO TELL YOU.

IT LOOKS LIKE MY INVESTIGATIONS POINT VERY HIGH. SO I'VE BEEN GIVEN THE ORDER TO BURY THIS CASE.

AND I'VE NO CHOICE BUT TO GIVE IN. THOSE BASTARDS KNOW WHERE TO SQUEEZE.

I'M OUT OF THE GAME, BUT NOT YOU. THIS IS MY PROPOSITION: ELIMINATE THAT MURDERING BASTARD AND I'LL PERSONALLY COVER YOUR BACK.

!

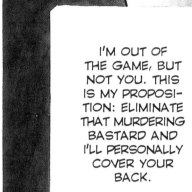

WHY ARE YOU DOING THIS, SMIRNOV?

I LIKE TO THINK OF A BETTER WORLD WHERE EVEN THE POWERFUL PAY THEIR DEBTS.

DEEP INSIDE, I AM NAÏVE.

EVEN AFTER WHAT HAPPENED, I WAS A LITTLE HAPPY. I WAS COMING BACK HOME, AND I HAD MADE A POWERFUL ALLY.

THE NEXT STEP SHOULD BE TO FIND THAT BULGING EYE FRIEND, BUT FIRST....

...A MUCH-NEEDED HOT SHOWER.

SUDDENLY, A CHILL AND THE SENSATION OF...

SURPRISE!

THE HOT SHOWER WOULD HAVE TO WAIT.

LET'S CLEAR SOMETHING, SIT DOWN AND BE QUIET.

PAF!

AW!

30

YOU AND I HAVE A COMPATIBILITY PROBLEM.

AND TO TELL YOU THE TRUTH, I DON'T HAVE THE INTENTION OF SHARING A SINGLE DOLLAR.

I'VE BEEN THAT BASTARD'S RIGHT HAND FOR TOO MANY YEARS. TOO MANY NOW FOR A SMART-ASS LIKE YOU TO COME AND TRY TO WIN MY HAND.

LOOK: I'VE GOT THE WEAPON THAT KILLED THAT BITCH WITH THE FINGERPRINTS OF HIS DIRTY FINGERS SIGNING THE CRIME.

AND YOU, WHAT DO YOU HAVE? THE GUN HE USED TO KILL LEON, MAYBE?

THE LIZARD WAS A BLACKMAILER, AND KNOWING THAT I WAS WORKING ALONE, HE THOUGHT THAT I ALSO WANTED TO MAKE MONEY FROM THE AFFAIR.

ANSWER!

31

39

THERE ARE A LOT OF CLICHÉS ABOUT US CATS. ONE SAYS THAT WE HAVE NINE LIVES.

THE TRUTH IS THAT I NEVER REALLY WANTED TO FIND OUT IF IT'S TRUE OR NOT.

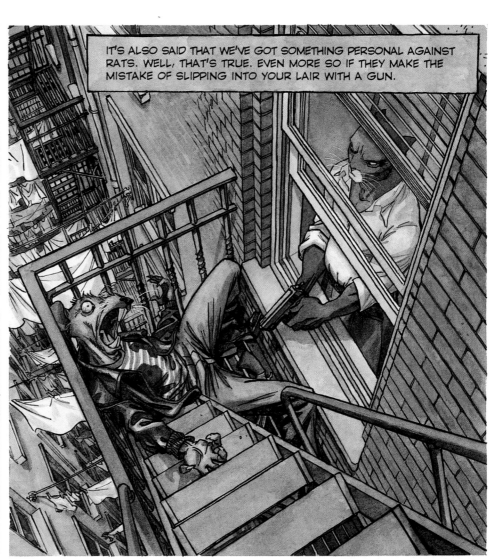

IT'S ALSO SAID THAT WE'VE GOT SOMETHING PERSONAL AGAINST RATS. WELL, THAT'S TRUE. EVEN MORE SO IF THEY MAKE THE MISTAKE OF SLIPPING INTO YOUR LAIR WITH A GUN.

WE ARE NOTHING... RIGHT, CAT?

SO MUCH TIME WAITING FOR MY CHANCE AND WHEN IT FINALLY HAPPENS, IT ALL FALLS TO PIECES....

I'VE ENDURED ALL KINDS OF HUMILIATIONS, BUT I ALWAYS THOUGHT ABOUT THE DAY WHEN I WOULD GET MY REVENGE....

HUH... NO THANKS, I DON'T SMOKE.

I GOT MY CHANCE WHEN *HE* STARTED SEEING THE ACTRESS.

EVERYTHING WAS GOING SMOOTHLY, IN THE MOST ABSOLUTE OF SILENCE, THE WAY *HE* HAD ORDERED IT. I WAS IN CHARGE OF DISCREETLY TAKING HER TO AND BACK FROM HER DATES, AVOIDING ALL PUBLICITY.

HOWEVER, BEING THE JEALOUS TYPE BY NATURE, *HE* HAD HIRED THE RAT TO SPY ON HER. APPARENTLY, SHE WASN'T A ONE-MAN WOMAN, UNFORTUNATELY FOR HER AND FOR LEON.

IT'S NOT VERY PLEASANT TO SEE SOMEONE DIE, AND EVEN LESS PLEASANT THE WAY HE DIED. I CAN STILL HEAR HIS SCREAMS. *HE* TOOK *HIS* TIME TO GIVE HIM THE "COUP DE GRÂCE".

34

WITH THE SAME COLD BLOOD *HE* PERSONALLY KILLED *HIS* GIRL.
WITHOUT A FLINCH, *HE* BLEW HER BRAINS OUT.

...BECAUSE *IVO STATOC* IS A SORE LOSER...

BUT I... LOOK AT ME... I'VE ALWAYS BEEN JUST A LOSER.

IVO STATOC.

SMIRNOV WASN'T WRONG. THE INVESTIGATIONS DID POINT VERY HIGH, INDEED.

SUCH AS THE LAST FLOOR OF THE STATOC TOWER, WHERE THE RICHEST GUY IN TOWN'S OFFICE WAS.

IVO STATOC, WAS ONE OF THOSE SELF-MADE MILLIONAIRES WHO DIDN'T CARE WHO THEY RUN OVER IN ORDER TO MAKE IT.

A PERSON USED TO ALL PRIVILEGES AND LACKING ANY MORAL STANDING.

ADAMS & MASSEY LAWYERS

STAFF ONLY

COME IN, COME IN MY FRIEND. BELIEVE ME, I ADMIRE YOU

A HANDYMAN IS WHAT I NEED. AND NOT ALL THOSE LOSERS AND INCOMPETENTS THAT SHOULD HAVE BEEN ABLE TO STOP YOU FROM GETTING HERE.

ANYWAY, AS YOU CAN SEE, I NEED NEW BLOOD....

PEOPLE LIKE YOU.

HEY, SON, WHAT ARE YOU THINKING? THAT'S NO WAY TO TREAT SOMEBODY WHO'S OFFERING YOU A JOB.

I DIDN'T COME HERE LOOKING FOR A JOB. IN FACT, MY FUTURE LOOKS BRIGHTER THAN YOURS.

48

YOU HAVE CLASS, BUT YOU'LL NEVER MAKE IT DRAGGING THAT LOAD.

YOU'RE MISSING THE MOST IMPORTANT THING, WHAT MAKES A GUY LIKE ME TO GET TO THE TOP ...

...COLD BLOOD.

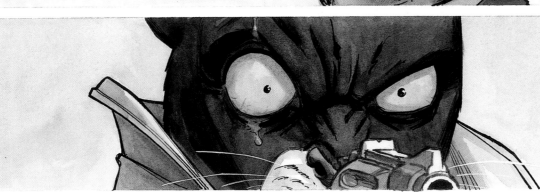

IF IT HADN'T BEEN FOR THAT SMIRK, I WOULD HAVE NOT BEEN ABLE TO KILL HIM, BUT THE HARM WAS ALREADY DONE. NOW HIS PRECIOUS COLD BLOOD WAS SPREADING ACROSS HIS DESK.

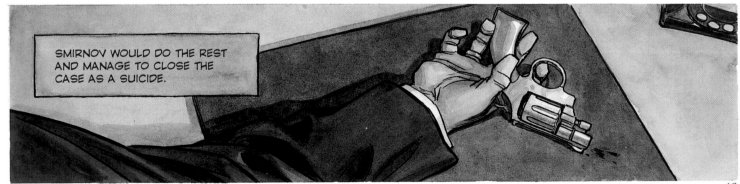

SMIRNOV WOULD DO THE REST AND MANAGE TO CLOSE THE CASE AS A SUICIDE.

42

PROBLEMS?

PCH! ROUTINE, A CONFRON- TATION...

I SEE.

WELL, GUYS. IS THIS THE GUY THAT HIT YOU AND YOU DECLARE TO HAVE...

... KILLED IVO STATOC. CONCENTRATE, TAKE YOUR TIME.

ITS HIM, THE FUCKING DETECTIVE.

HE'S THE KILLER!

COUIC!

TOUGH LUCK, GUYS. THIS MAN'S GOT AN ALIBI: HE WAS IN HIS APARTMENT WHEN ALL THIS HAPPENED. THE LIEUTENANT HERE WAS WATCHING HIM SINCE HE WAS CONSIDERED A SUSPECT IN THE WILFORD MURDER. ISN'T THAT RIGHT, LIEUTENANT?

NOW, NOW... THOSE REMARKS WON'T GET YOU ANYWHERE.

YEP.

SON OF A BITCH!

THAT'S NOT TRUE, LYING BASTARDS! IT'S ALL A SET-UP!

44

LIEUTENANT, GO ON WITH THE IN-TERROGATION. EITHER I'M MISTAKEN OR OUR FRIENDS HERE KNOW A LOT MORE ABOUT THE DEATHS OF NATALIA WILFORD AND LEON KRONSKI.

O.K.

THIS IS A JOKE!

FUCKERS!

I WANT TO TALK TO MY LAWYER!

THE TRUTH IS, JOHN... THAT I USED TO SEE CLEARLY, BUT NOW...

...ANYWAY, WHAT I'M TRYING TO SAY IS THAT I'M NOT TOO PROUD OF MYSELF. I DON'T HAVE A CLEAN CONSCIENCE, AND IT'S A VERY UN-PLEASANT FEELING.

45

4117

JUANJO GUARNIDO & JUAN DÍAZ CANALES · 2000

JuanDíaz
CANALES

Juanjo
GUARNIDO

JUAN DÍAZ CANALES was born in Madrid, Spain, in 1972. Canales began reading comics when he was a child. At the age of 18, he enrolled in a school for animation where he met Juanjo Guarnido with whom he formed a close friendship. They continued to stay in contact after Guarnido left to work for the Disney animation studios in France, sharing their thoughts and concepts for a comic book project that would take form under the name of *Blacksad*, a series written by Canales in the strong style of the hard-boiled detective novels and films of the Thirties.

Together with three designers, Canales formed in 1996 the studio named Trident Animation which did work for numerous American and European companies. During this time Canales worked on *Blacksad* and assorted animation projects for film and television. Canales presently lives in Madrid, Spain.

Blacksad is his first graphic novel. It won the Avenir prize for best new talent in November 2000 at the Lys-lez-Lanois festival, and in 2001 at the international comics festival at Angoulême, *Blacksad* was nominated for the Coup de Coeur award.

JUANJO GUARNIDO was born in Grenada, Spain, in 1967. He studied at the School of Fine Arts in Grenada where he obtained his diploma. During those years he had a number of illustrations published in *Comics Forum*, a magazine produced by Planeta de Agostini that featured Spanish-language versions of Marvel Comics stories. From there he worked three years in Madrid doing animation work for television.

In 1993, he moved to Paris, France, where he began work at the Walt Disney Studios in Montreuil, where he worked as a layout man before becoming an animator.

Blacksad is his first graphic novel.

Guarnido has won numerous international awards for his artwork including the award for the best new graphic album (*Blacksad*) in the festival at Lys-lez-Lannois in 2000. *Blacksad* was also nominated for the Coup de Coeur award at the international comics festival at Angoulême. He presently lives in Paris, France.